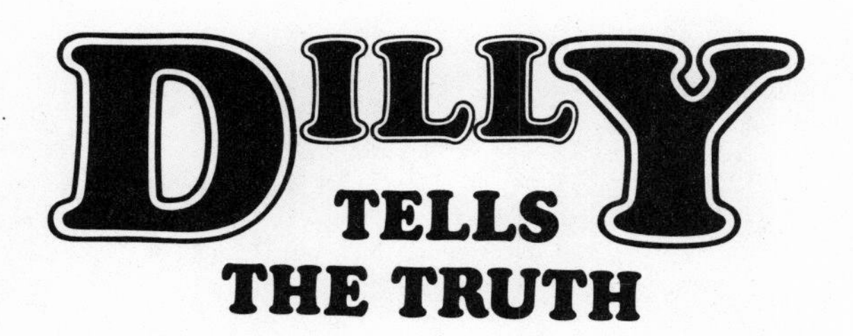
DILLY
TELLS
THE TRUTH

TONY BRADMAN

DILLY TELLS THE TRUTH

Illustrated by Susan Hellard

Viking Kestrel

VIKING KESTREL
Published by the Penguin Group
Viking Penguin Inc., 40 West 23rd Street, New York, New York 10010, U.S.A.
Penguin Books Ltd, 27 Wrights Lane, London W8 5TZ, England
Penguin Books Australia Ltd, Ringwood, Victoria, Australia
Penguin Books Canada Ltd, 2801 John Street, Markham, Ontario, Canada L3R 1B4
Penguin Books (N.Z.) Ltd, 182-190 Wairau Road, Auckland 10, New Zealand

Penguin Books Ltd, Registered Offices: Harmondsworth, Middlesex, England

First published in Great Britain by Piccadilly Press Ltd., 1987

First American edition published in 1988

1 3 5 7 9 10 8 6 4 2

Library of Congress Cataloging in Publication Data
Bradman, Tony. Dilly tells the truth
by Tony Bradman ; illustrated by Susan Hellard. p. cm.
Summary: Dilly the naughty little dinosaur comes down with the
measles, decides to tell the exact truth regardless of repercussions,
holds his own Dinolympics in the back yard, and gets lost on a family outing.
ISBN 0–670–82350–3
[1. Dinosaurs—Fiction.] I. Hellard, Susan, ill. II. Title.
PZ7.B7275Dhv 1988 [Fic]—dc19 88–14234 CIP
Printed in the United States of America by Haddon Craftsmen, Bloomsburg, Pennsylvania

CONTENTS

I. DILLY AND THE MEDICINE 1

II. DILLY TELLS THE TRUTH 16

III. DILLY AND THE GOLD MEDAL 24

IV. DILLY GETS LOST 36

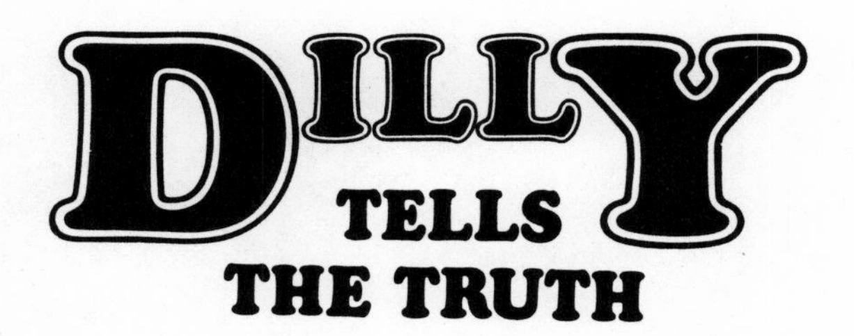
DILLY
TELLS
THE TRUTH

I. Dilly and the Medicine

The other day, I was in my room reading my favorite book, *The Famous Five Dinosaurs,* when Mother came in to see me. She looked worried.

"Have you seen Dilly?" she said.

Dilly's my little brother. Mother, Father and I all love Dilly—but sometimes he can be so naughty.

"No, Mother," I said. "I haven't seen him since you yelled at him." Dilly had wanted to help Mother in the garden, but he had pulled up Father's best swamp lilies again, so Mother had sent him indoors.

"Well," she said, "he's been very quiet since then. He's been acting very strangely today, too. He didn't drink his pineapple juice at breakfast this morning, and that's not like him at all."

It's true, that wasn't like Dilly. If there's one thing he loves more than anything else, it's his pineapple juice.

Mother asked me to help her find Dilly, and we looked all over the house. But he was nowhere to be found. He certainly wasn't

anywhere we expected him to be, like inside the cupboards he wasn't supposed to open, or rummaging through the trash, or climbing

up to get at the sugar cane jar in the kitchen.

Mother was looking really worried.

"Now where can that dinosaur be?" she said.

Just then I heard a sound coming from Dilly's room.

"Urrff urrff," went the sound. "Urrff urrff."

Mother looked at me, and I looked at Mother.

"You don't suppose Dilly could be in his room," I said. "It's the only place we haven't tried yet."

But Mother didn't say anything. She was already on her way up the stairs. I followed her, and when we opened the door to Dilly's room we saw . . . Dilly, lying on his bed.

Mother was very angry.

"Dilly Dinosaur," she said, "what do you think you're doing? It's not bedtime yet, and if I've told you once, I've told you a thousand times that you're not to mess up your bed . . . and you've still got your muddy shoes on! Oh Dilly, you are *such* a bad dinosaur!"

It was strange, though. Dilly wasn't acting like he normally does. Usually when he's told off he starts arguing back, or he sulks, or lets loose with a 150-mile-per-hour ultra-special super-scream. But he was just lying there looking sorry for himself. I could see that he looked all hot and sweaty, too.

And then Dilly did something *very* strange.

"I'm sorry, Mother," he said. It came out all croaky, so I wasn't sure

I'd heard him right at first.

"What did you say, Dilly?" Mother asked him.

"I'm sorry, Mother," he said again. It wasn't quite so croaky this time, but it did sound as if there was something wrong with Dilly's voice. I was more surprised that he was saying sorry, though. That was something Dilly hardly ever did!

Mother was surprised too.

"Are you sure you're feeling all right, Dilly?" she said. She sat down on the bed next to him and felt his head. "You feel very hot . . . and your voice sounds funny. Does it hurt? Is your throat sore?"

Dilly shook his head. Mother looked hard at him.

"Dilly Dinosaur," she said, "if you don't feel well you must tell me."

Dilly just shook his head again and said nothing.

"If Dilly is sick," I said, "does that mean he won't be able to go to Dixie's party tomorrow?"

Now Dixie is Dilly's best friend, and she had invited him to her birthday party. He had been looking forward to it for ages.

"Oh," said Mother, with a smile on her face, "I see. You won't admit that you don't feel well because you don't want to miss Dixie's party. Well, Dilly, I'm afraid that if you *are* sick then you'll have to miss it."

I could see that Dilly looked really upset.

"I'm not sick!" he said in his croaky voice. He sat up and got off his bed.

Mother looked hard at him.

"Okay, Dilly," she said. "Have it your way. But I'm going to keep an eye on you today, and if you are sick, I'm afraid you probably won't be able to go to the party. Why, someone might catch what you've got! You don't want to make all your friends sick too, do you?"

I could see that Dilly was thinking about that, and that he wanted to say something . . . but he didn't. He coughed instead.

"Urrff urrff," he went. "URRFF URRFF!"

Dilly tried to keep going, but by lunchtime his cough sounded really bad. By the middle of the afternoon he didn't look well at all, and by the evening he looked terrible. But he wouldn't admit that he felt sick.

He wouldn't admit it even when

he started to break out in spots. He
was still trying to argue when
Mother got him into his pajamas
and put him to bed.

"Let's have no more nonsense
now, Dilly," she said. "It looks to me
like you've got something someone
might catch!"

Dilly didn't say anything. But he'd
become pale green, and I could
see little yellow spots all over him.

A little while later, I heard Mother talking to the doctor on the dino-phone.

"Yes, Doctor," she was saying. "I know he bit you the last time you saw him, but I think he was frightened . . . oh, you're frightened of *him* . . . but you will come, won't you? He really isn't very well . . ."

The doctor did come in the end. Dilly behaved himself and did everything the doctor asked him to. I think he still thought that if he were good, he might get to go to Dixie's party after all. But the doctor said that he had measles, and that he would be very infectious for a few days. He also gave Mother some green medicine in a bottle for Dilly to take.

Now if there's one thing that Dilly hates, it's taking medicine. Usually when he has to have some, he shuts his mouth up very tight and won't open it at all. And if Mother or Father try to make him take it, he shouts and screams and is as naughty as he can be.

But today he wasn't as worried about the medicine as about whether he could go to Dixie's party.

"Come on now, Dilly," said Mother after the doctor had gone. "It's time to take your medicine. It will help you get better."

"Can I go to Dixie's party if I take my medicine?" Dilly said in his very croaky voice.

"I'm sorry, Dilly," said Mother, "but you can't go to the party. The doctor says you've got to stay in for at least a week. Now come on, take your medicine, there's a good dinosaur . . ."

Mother poured the medicine into a spoon and held it out toward Dilly. Dilly looked at it, and then he opened his mouth for a 150-mile-per-hour, ultra-special super-scream . . . but nothing came out. His croaky voice had finally gone altogether!

Dilly was so surprised that he forgot to close his mouth, and Mother popped the medicine in before he even knew what was happening. Dilly swallowed, but he looked very, very mad.

"Dilly," said Mother, "I know you wanted to go to the party. But there will be other parties, and you really must admit it if you don't feel well. Now you lie down and go to sleep." She gave him a kiss, and told him to snuggle down.

The medicine must have been very good, because Dilly was a little better the next day, and much better by the day after that.

He stayed in bed, but on the third day he began to get bored. He drew some pictures, and I played with him for a while. But what he wanted most of all was plenty of pineapple juice—and for Mother and Father to read him his favorite books over and over again.

"Which one now, Dilly?" I heard Father say. "*The Bad Dinosaurs' Counting Book? Where the Dinosaurs Are? Dinolocks and the Three Bears?* I'm not reading *Dinorella* again, that's for sure."

And when Dilly heard that, he screamed. It wasn't a real Dilly scream, though—it was still a little croaky and wobbly.

"I hear Dilly's got his voice back," said Mother, looking around the bedroom door.

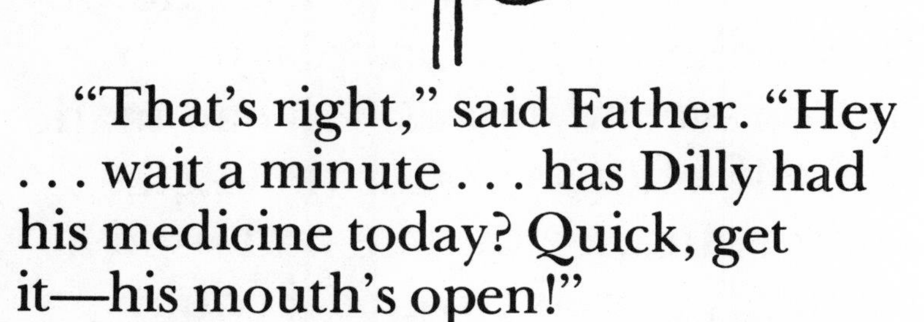

"That's right," said Father. "Hey . . . wait a minute . . . has Dilly had his medicine today? Quick, get it—his mouth's open!"

And do you know, when Dilly heard Father say that, he stopped screaming right away . . . and we all laughed.

Including Dilly!

II. DILLY TELLS THE TRUTH

The other day, when I came home from school, Dilly was playing one of his favorite games. He had made himself a house under the table, and I could see that he had used a lot of my things to do it. I could even see the feet of my best plateosaurus doll sticking out.

"Dilly," I said, "have you got my doll under there? My best doll, the one I got for my birthday?"

There was no answer.

"Dilly," I said, "I know you've got my doll, and I want it back."

"I haven't got your doll."

"But I can see it. I want it back," I shouted.

Just then, Mother came into the kitchen.

"What's all this noise?" she asked. "Why are you shouting at each other?"

"Dilly's got my best birthday doll," I said, "and I want it back."

Mother looked under the table.

"Dilly? Have you got Dorla's doll? You know you should give the doll back when your sister's home."

There was no answer.

"Dilly says he hasn't got my doll," I said. "But he has, I saw it, so he's telling *lies*."

Now if there's one thing that Mother really can't stand, it's a child who tells a lie.

"Dilly Dinosaur," she said, in a very angry voice, "you come out this minute."

Dilly wriggled out of his under-the-table house.

"Have you, or have you not got your sister's doll there?" said Mother.

Dilly looked down.

"Well?"

Dilly started to cry.

"Yes," he said. "But I want to play with it."

"You're a very bad dinosaur, Dilly," said Mother. "You have told a lie, and I don't know how many times I've told you that you must always tell the truth."

Dilly sniffed.

"Now you are to give the doll back to your sister, and then you are to neaten up all your toys like a good dinosaur," said Mother. "And Dilly . . ."

"Yes, Mother?" said Dilly, looking around.

"Just you remember that you must always tell the truth."

"Yes, Mother," he said. "I'll remember."

The next day was a very special one, because we were going to see Grandma and Grandpa. They don't live very far away, and they're always pleased to see us. When we arrived, Grandma said that we were to sit down at the table right away.

"I've made you a marshberry cake," she said. "I know it's your favorite."

Grandma makes delicious cakes, and this was one of her best. We had coconuts, and mosquito tarts, and swamp fruit and drinks of pineapple juice, too.

When we had all finished, Grandpa leaned back in his chair and patted his front.

"I'm so full I feel as if I could burst," he said.

Dilly looked at him.

"You're very fat, Grandpa," he said. Grandpa just laughed, but Father was angry.

"Dilly Dinosaur," said Father, "what a thing to say! You shouldn't say such rude things to your Grandpa."

Dilly looked confused.

"But Mother said I should always tell the truth," he said. "And Grandpa *is* rather fat."

Grandpa laughed again.

"Dilly's got a point there, you know," he said. "I suppose I ought to go on a diet and get rid of some of this weight."

"But then you wouldn't be so cuddly anymore," said Mother. "And Dilly likes to sit on your lap for a cuddle."

"That's true," said Grandpa. "Well, what do you think, Dilly? Should I have the last piece of Grandma's marshberry cake and stay fat, or should I go on a diet and get all bony and thin?"

Dilly looked serious for a second.

"I know," he said. "I'll eat the marshberry cake, then Grandma can make another one. And Grandpa and I will eat that too, and we'll both get fat and cuddly." Dilly smiled his biggest smile.

"But if you get too fat, Dilly," said Mother, "you won't be able to bend down and pick up your toys when it's time to neaten up."

"Oh," said Dilly. He was thoughtful for a moment. Then he said, "Can we have another marshberry cake then, Grandma?"

Everyone laughed.

"What a bad dinosaur you are, Dilly," said Mother, smiling.

"But at least I tell the truth now," said Dilly.

"You certainly do, Dilly," said Grandpa. "You certainly do."

III. Dilly and the Gold Medal

I love watching sports on TV. Best of all I like to watch athletics. I love to see all those fast dinosaurs racing, and those big dinosaurs throwing giant ferns and rocks as far as they can, or seeing who can wallow in a swamp the longest, and those tall dinosaurs doing the giant fern jump.

So you can imagine how excited I was the other day when I found out what was happening. It was the first day of the Dinolympics, which meant that all the best dinosaur athletes in the world would be racing and throwing and jumping together. And it was all going to be on TV!

Mother and Father were almost as excited as I was, because they like sports too. In fact we could hardly wait for the program to begin.

"Come on, Dilly," said Father. "It's almost time for the first race to start."

Dilly looked confused.

"What race, Father?" he said.

"The first race in the Dinolympics, silly Dilly," I said. "Don't you know anything?"

"Now, now, Dorla," said Father. "That's not very nice . . . I'm sure you didn't understand such things as the Dinolympics when you were Dilly's age."

"What's a Dino . . . Dino . . . limpet?" asked Dilly.

"It's Dinolympics, Dilly," said Father. "It's when all the best athletes in the world get together to see who can run the fastest, throw things the farthest, and jump the highest. It's really exciting."

"And they get prizes, too," I said.

Now if there's one thing that Dilly loves, it's winning a prize. Whenever he goes to a party where they have games, Dilly tries so hard to win one that he almost forgets to be naughty. So as soon as I said prizes, I could see that he was very interested in the Dinolympics.

"What sort of prizes do they get?" he said.

"Well," said Father, "they get special medals. A bronze medal if you're third, a silver if you're second, and a beautiful gold medal if you're first."

I could see that Dilly liked the sound of that.

"Can I enter a race, Father?" he asked. "I want a gold medal."

Father laughed.

"It's not quite that simple," said Father. "You have to practice very hard, and eat up all your swamp greens, and it takes a long time to become as strong or as fast as the best dinosaurs in the world. But I'm sure that if you really want to, Dilly, you could be a champion at something too."

"I'll bet he could be the world's champion bad dinosaur," I said.

"Now that's enough of that, Dorla," said Father. "Look . . . the first race is starting!"

We watched the Dinolympics on TV a lot over the next few weeks. We really enjoyed it, and Dilly liked it so much that it became his favorite game. Even after the Dinolympics were finished, Dilly still wanted to play racing. He made me or Mother or Father help him, too – but only to start him off.

"You have to say ready, set, go," he would say, "and then I race and I win and you give me a gold medal."

"But what if you aren't the winner?" said Mother one day.

Dilly looked confused.

"But I'm always the winner," he said.

"That's because you don't race against anybody else," said Mother. "You might not be the winner if you had someone to race against."

I could see that Dilly didn't like the idea of not being the winner.

To help Dilly enjoy his game a little more, Father made him a gold medal from some cardboard, gold paper, and string. Dilly was really pleased with it. Mother found him a box so that he could stand on it while she hung it around his neck, just like the winning dinosaurs did at the Dinolympics when they got their medals.

Dilly loved his gold medal. He wore it all the time, and he didn't even want to take it off when he took a bath or went to bed, but Mother and Father said he had to. He kept it under his pillow at night, and in the morning, the first thing he did was to put it on.

A few days later, Dixie came to play. Now Dilly loves Dixie. She's just about his favorite friend, and he gets so excited when she comes to our house that he's almost always naughty in one way or another.

But on this particular day, he wasn't naughty to begin with. Dixie had brought her new Dino-trike with her to show Dilly, and he was so interested in it that he was very well behaved. That didn't last long, though, and he was just about to try and push Dixie off her Dino-trike when she noticed Dilly's medal.

"What's that around your neck, Dilly?" she asked.

"That's my gold medal," said Dilly, proudly. "I got it for winning a race."

"It's lovely and shiny," said Dixie.

"I wish I had a gold medal."

Dilly smiled.

"Well, you can't have mine," he said.

Dilly and Dixie played with the Dino-trike for a while longer. Then Mother came out into the yard.

"Why don't you play racing with Dixie?" she said to Dilly. "Now's your chance to have a real race with someone."

Mother smiled, but I could see that Dilly didn't like the idea. Dixie

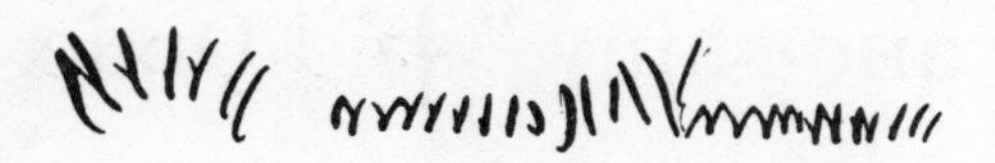

did, though.

"Oh, yes," she said. "And if I win, can I have the gold medal?"

Dilly opened his mouth, but Mother spoke before he had a chance to say anything.

"Oh, I should think so," she said, laughing. "Okay . . . now, the first to the giant fern is the winner . . . ready, set . . . GO!" she said.

Dilly and Dixie raced across the lawn and back again . . . and Dixie won, but only just barely.

"I won! I won!" she said. "I get the gold medal!"

"It's not fair," said Dilly. "I wasn't ready!" I could see Dilly looked really upset.

"Oh Dilly," said Mother. "Okay, why don't you see who can jump the farthest? They do that at the Dinolympics, don't they? Here, you can take a long run, jump from here where the swamp lilies are, and I'll measure who does the biggest jump. Off you go!"

Dixie did her jump first. She ran up as fast as she could, jumped . . . and went such a long way! Mother was very impressed.

"That's very, very good, Dixie," said Mother. "Come on, Dilly, it's your turn now!"

Dilly tried as hard as he could . . .

but it was no good. His jump was just a tiny bit shorter than Dixie's.

Dilly had lost again. He looked really upset, and stomped off toward the house, stomp, stomp, stomp.

"Does that mean I get the gold medal?" Dixie asked Mother.

Mother opened her mouth, but Dilly turned around and spoke before she had a chance to say anything.

"I bet I can do one thing better than Dixie," he said.

"What's that, Dilly?" said Mother.

Dilly didn't answer her. Instead, he opened his mouth . . . and let rip an ultra-special, 150-mile-per-hour super-scream, the sort that makes Dixie dive for cover in the bushes, me run into the house, and Mother hide behind the giant fern. When he'd finished, Mother told him off and sent him indoors.

Later, when Dilly was in bed, he said he was sorry for being so bad. He also said that he was going to give his gold medal to Dixie.

"Why's that, Dilly?" said Mother.

"Well, she did beat me," he said. "She was the winner."

"But who would be the winner if there was . . . a screaming contest?"

Mother asked.

"I would," smiled Dilly.

"That's right . . . because you've got the loudest, the biggest, the best scream in the world," said Mother, laughing. "Not that I want to hear it all that often."

Dilly smiled, and went to sleep.

And later, Father and I made another gold medal, so that Dilly and Dixie could have one each. I think they both deserved one . . . don't you?

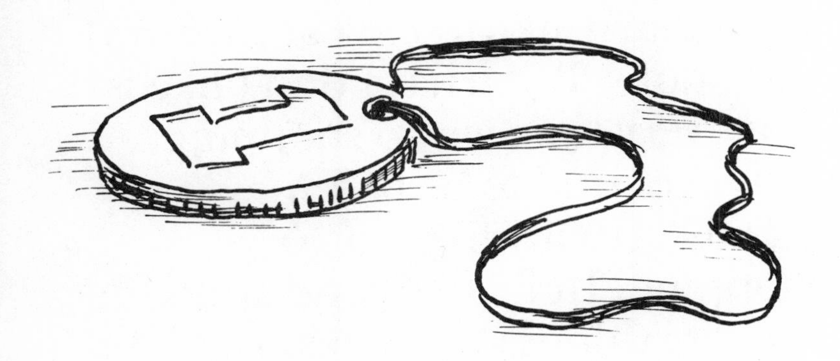

IV. Dilly Gets Lost

Usually on the weekend we have to go shopping, and that's something I hate. It isn't that I don't like looking around big stores . . . I do. I particularly like to look at the toys and books. But what I don't like is that every time we go shopping, Dilly is bound to be bad.

Dilly actually likes to go shopping. In fact, it's one of his favorite things . . . especially if

Mother and Father buy him what he wants. If they don't, well, Dilly often throws a tantrum. And one of Dilly's tantrums is enough to spoil anyone's day!

So last Saturday I wasn't surprised to hear Father having a word with Dilly before we left to go shopping.

"Now Dilly," he was saying, "I hope you're going to be a good dinosaur today."

"I'll be good, Father," said Dilly.

Father gave him a hard look.

"Do you promise me that you won't be naughty?" he asked.

Dilly smiled one of his biggest I'm-going-to-be-as-good-as-I-can-be smiles.

"I promise, Father," he said.

"And do you promise that you

won't throw a tantrum and roll around on the floor like you did the last time we went shopping?" said Father.

"Yes, Father," said Dilly. "I mean no, Father, I won't do that."

Father gave him another hard look. And then he smiled.

"Okay, Dilly," he said. "I believe you."

But I didn't believe Dilly at all.

Anyway, not long after that, we all climbed into the Dino-car and set off to do our shopping.

It was very crowded in the streets and the big stores when we got there.

"Dilly, you hold on to Father," said Mother, "and Dorla, you hold on to me. We don't want you getting lost. Don't run off, Dilly."

"No, Mother," said Dilly. We both did what she said.

Dilly was also very well behaved —to begin with. The first thing we did was to go to the supermarket, where we got a few things that we needed. We bought plenty of fern stalks and swamp greens, and some fern flakes and roots for breakfast.

"I think that's about it," said Father, looking at his list.

“Don’t forget my pineapple juice, Father,” said Dilly.

Father smiled.

“You’re right to remind us, Dilly,” he said. “We do need some more pineapple juice. What a good dinosaur you’re being today . . . although sometimes I wish you’d drink a little less pineapple juice. It’s costing us a fortune!”

We all laughed, and Dilly popped two cartons of pineapple juice into the shopping basket.

It took us ages to get out of the supermarket because of the lines at the checkout. Then we went to buy some shoes for Father. After that, Mother wanted to go and buy some material. Finally, we were finished and Mother and Father said they had a treat in store for us.

"Because you've both been so good and helpful this morning," said Mother, "we thought we'd buy you a little present each . . ."

". . . And then go for a fern-burger at MacDinosaur's!"

Dilly looked at me . . . and I looked at Dilly.

And we both shouted . . .

"Hooray!"

Choosing a present was easy. Both Dilly and I asked if we could have a book, and I got *The Famous Five Dinosaurs Go Swamp-Wallowing*. Dilly got *The Very Hungry Dinosaur.*

"That's a good choice for a Dinosaur who's going for a fern-burger," laughed Father. "Are you hungry, Dilly?"

Dilly didn't say anything. He just

nodded as hard as he could. He was still nodding when we got to MacDinosaur's. It was very, very crowded there, more crowded than anywhere else we'd been.

"That's lucky," said Father. "There's a table . . . okay, you sit down and I'll go and get the food. Now, what do you all want . . . Dorla?"

I wanted just an ordinary fern-burger and a cola. Mother asked for the same.

"And what about you, Dilly?" asked Father.

Dilly didn't say anything for a moment. Then he looked up at Father and smiled.

"I'm a very, very, very hungry dinosaur," he said, "and I want a Bronto-burger and french fries and a Triple-Dipple Dino-shake."

"Now Dilly," said Father, "I think that's a little too much for a dinosaur your age. Those Bronto-burgers are pretty big . . . why, I don't think even I could manage one, even without french fries and a Triple-Dipple Dino-shake."

"But it's what I want," said Dilly, very quietly.

"Well, you're going to have to choose something else, I'm afraid," said Father. I could see that he was beginning to look angry. It was hot and noisy and other dinosaurs kept bumping into him.

"I want a Bronto-burger," said Dilly, quietly. He had his most stubborn face on.

"I'm sorry, Dilly," said Father, "but you're not having one."

I looked at Dilly, and I could see

that he was really mad. And usually, when Dilly gets mad, he lets loose with an ultra-special, 150-mile-per-hour super-scream. At the very least I expected him to have a tantrum and roll around on the floor.

But he didn't. He did something very different instead.

"I hate you!" he shouted at Father . . . and then he ran off into the crowd. He did it so quickly that none of us could stop him.

"Dilly!" shouted Mother. "You come back this instant!"

Father ran after him, but it was too late. Dilly had completely disappeared.

Father went to talk to the manager of MacDinosaur's while Mother and I stayed at the table, in case Dilly should come back. Soon we heard an announcement being made from a loudspeaker.

"Please look out for a small dinosaur who has lost his parents. He is wearing purple jeans and answers to the name of Dilly . . ." and then there was a lot of crackling.

Father came back to the table, and then Mother went off to look for Dilly. I could tell that they were both very worried. I was worried too . . . I know that Dilly can be bad. I know that sometimes he spoils my games and makes me mad. But he's still my little brother, and I love him, and I didn't want him to be lost.

And now he was nowhere to be found.

Mother came back to our table. She looked as if she were going to cry.

"I can't see him anywhere," she started to say. "I think we'd better get the Dino-Police . . ."

But she didn't finish what she was saying. In fact everyone in MacDinosaur's became very quiet when they heard the noise that came next.

It was an ultra-special, 150-mile-per-hour super-scream,

the sort that makes Father dive under the table, me hide under a chair, and Mother turn bright green with embarrassment.

It was Dilly, of course. At first we couldn't tell where he was, although from the sound of his super-scream we knew he must be somewhere close. It turned out that he hadn't run very far, and that he had hidden under a table only a little way from ours. Father grabbed Dilly, who was still screaming, and we all ran out.

Mother and Father gave him such a yelling at when we got home. They told him that running off was the silliest thing he could do, and also the most dangerous. They sent him straight to his room and made him stay there for the rest of the day. And I was really mad because I had to go without my fern-burger.

Later on, though, at bedtime, I heard Father talking to Dilly.

"You really were very naughty today," he was saying. "You had us all very worried . . . and why did you scream like that?"

"I got frightened, Father," said Dilly. "I didn't like being on my own and I wanted you to find me."

Father laughed.

"Well," he said, "you certainly chose the best way of helping us. I'll tell you a secret, too, Dilly . . . that's the first time I've ever been really glad to hear you scream!"

I could see that Dilly was smiling.

Father made Dilly promise that he would never run off like that again. Dilly said that he was going to try and be good all the time from now on, too.

I think he'll keep his promise not to run away and get lost. But do you think he'll be able to stop himself from being bad sometimes?

We'll just have to wait and see!